CAMPIN' CHAOS!

THE
DOG DIARIES
SERIES

DOG DIARIES

When the evil Miss Stricker accuses Junior of being a BAD DOG, Ruff and Junior have to attend obedience classes to get him out of trouble...

HAPPY HOWLIDAYS!

From Fangs Giving and Crisp-Mouth to the mysterious Saint Lick, follow Junior on the poochiest, most barktastic adventure through the Howliday Season!

MISSION IMPAWSIBLE

Junior is going to Hollywood! But when the vacation with his best mutt-mates takes a VERY unexpected turn, he'll need to find a way to escape a LIVING NIGHTMARE!

CURSE OF THE MYSTERY MUTT

Something terrible is going on in Hills Village... Can Junior find the evil mastermind who is TERRIER-izing the town?

DOG DIARIES

STEVEN BUTLER

CAMPING CHAOS!

AND JAMES PATTERSON

Illustrated by
RICHARD WATSON

1 3 5 7 9 10 8 6 4 2

Young Arrow
20 Vauxhall Bridge Road
London SW1V 2SA

Young Arrow is part of the Penguin Random House group of companies
whose addresses can be found at global.penguinrandomhouse.com

Penguin
Random House
UK

First published in Great Britain by Young Arrow in 2020

www.penguin.co.uk

A CIP catalogue record for this book is available from the British Library

ISBN 9781529119787

Printed and bound in Great Britain by
Clays Ltd, Elcograf S.p.A.

Penguin Random House is committed to a sustainable future for our
business, our readers and our planet. This book is made from Forest
Stewardship Council® certified paper.

*For the BARKTASTIC
pupils and teachers of Farfield
Primary and Nursery School
in Bradford*

– S.B.

I have one word for you, my person-pal…
WE'RE GOING ON VACATION!

Okay…okay…that was four words, I
know, but I'm just a little over-excited right
now and I can't help it! My ears are twitchy,
my jowls are drooly, and I'm giving serious
thought to spending the entire afternoon
having one long HIP-HOORAY-HOUNDY-
HOWL!

Let me explain…Right now, my amazing
furless person-pack of humans, THE

CATCH-A-DOGGY-BONE PACK, and I are about to clamber into the moving people-box on wheels and head out of Hills Village, hitting the road for a really real surprise adventure!

I wonder what it'll be! Where in the world is Mom-Lady taking us? AGH! I'M SO EXCITED! I've been waiting for the chance to go on the vacation of a lifetime for… well…A LIFETIME! HA HA!

My best buddy, Ruff, and I are bound to have the most amazing time, I just know it, and the thought of vacationing with him has made my tail waggier than EVER! Make no mistake, I have the most terrific pet human in all of Hills Village. No, scratch that…the world! No, scratch that…THE UNIVERSE!

~~RAFE~~
Ruff

~~MOM~~
Mom-Lady

~~GEORGIA~~
Jawjaw

~~JUNIOR~~ Me!

3

Ruff makes me want to yip-yap with joy and do a Happy Dance from daybreak to snooze time, and now…we're finally getting the chance to snuffle off into the sunset together for a whole week of playing ball, nose-boops, snacking, and snoozing! It's going to be bliss.

Well…umm…I'm sure it is. Mom-Lady has been super-secretive about where we're actually heading, but I can tell she's giddy as a greyhound who just stole Grandmoo's slipper, so it has to be great!

But I'm getting ahead of myself…

Introductions are extremely important to us pooches. And I'd say it's time for ours.

If we've already met and you've read my AMAZING Dog Diaries before…Welcome back, my person-pal! I'm so happy you decided to come along for another spot of masterful mischief!

If you've never pawed through any of my mutt manuals before, however, then I should probably start by telling you that I'm Junior...Junior Catch-A-Doggy-Bone... HELLO! It's a pleasure to sniff you!

I should also try to shed a little light on some of the BARKTASTIC and FUR-RAISING things that have happened to me since I came to live in the Catch-A-Doggy-Bone kennel, or you'll have no idea what I'm barking on about.

Y'see, I've had my fair share of crazy scrapes with obedience classes, canine criminals, midnight feasts, stolen treasured trinkets, junkyard hijinks, terrifying turkeys, dandy-dog shows, howly wieners, vicious vacuum cleaners, and bowlfuls of Meaty-Giblet-Jumble-Chum. But one of the most spine-jangling, MOST HOUNDY HEART-POUNDING moments of all, was the time I thought we were going on vacation to HOLLYWOOD! Sounds terrific, right? WRONG!

I tell you, my person-pal, I couldn't have been more excited to bark my way along the boulevards of Tinkletown (I think that's what they call it) and snuffle through those streets paved with sausage meat. So you can imagine how horrified I was when it all went totally bonkers and my pooch-pack and I ended up in a hotel for…for…This isn't easy to say. We ended up in a hotel for…VEGETARIAN DOGS!

OH, THE TERROR!

I don't want to ruin that story for you in case you haven't read it, and I certainly don't want to spend even one more second talking about that VEG-O-RIFFIC disaster. Ugh! Just the thought of it makes me shudder.

It goes without saying that this mangey mutt is definitely in need of his first ever dream vacation without any of the vexation. Ha ha!

Yep! A little me-time to stretch my paws and feel the wind in my tail is just what the veterinarian ordered…and now it's finally happening!

It started two days ago. C'mon…I'll tell you all about it.

Last Friday

It was already a great day, my person-pal. After all the creepy craziness of Howly Wiener, and the barky bedlam of the Howliday Season, I was so happy that spring had rolled its way across Hills Village.

Don't get me wrong…there isn't a dog anywhere who doesn't adore the winter-time. What's not to love?! Who could be unhappy with snow to run through and Carol singing (whoever Carol is!), turkey treats to taste, parties, and extra-long cozy snuggles with your pet humans? BUT… when spring is here, our sniff-a-licious senses start tingling and we know it's time to get SUPER busy.

Let me explain…

Of all the seasons of the year, spring is definitely the most hectic for a dog like me. After the winter snow has melted and vanished, there's serious work to be done.

While you human-types dive head-first into cleaning and sorting and organizing for the new year ahead, us mutts get on with the serious stuff. Every tree, trash can, and mailbox from here to the far side of Hills Village needs to be re-scented and sniffed. There are backyards to be re-pooped and garden gates that need to be peed on. Delicious old bones from last summer need to be dug up and chewed, fences need scratching, the bushes in the dog park need to be re-explored, and…and…this is the most exciting part, my furless friend. It's hard for me to say without throwing my head back and bow-wowing like a pup at playtime…ALL THE NEIGHBORHOOD RACCOONS COME OUT OF THEIR DENS!!!

If there's one thing I am an expert in, it's barking at raccoons. It's my favorite houndy-hobby and a very important part of my daily schedule. I'm practically the INTERNATIONAL MUTT MASTER of kicking up a raccoon racket.

IT'S TRUE! If I were a superhero like the ones in Ruff's Captain Chaos comic books, it would be my best-best-BESTEST power of all.

I can't describe how much I love howling and yowling as I guard the trash cans from those stinky little fluff-balls. It's in the top ten of my absolute favorite things…

JUNIOR'S TOP 10 FAVORITE THINGS

10. Raccoons!
9. Practicing my raccoon bark on the mailman
8. Chewing socks from the laundry pile
7. Thinking about barking at raccoons
6. My pooch-pals
5. Sniffing for raccoons
4. A full doggy bowl
3. Sleeping, snoozing and drooling
2. Chasing raccoons
1. Ruff, Ruff and more Ruff…sigh … and RACCOONS!

See what I mean? I swear, I could go on and on about raccoons…raccoooooons… RACCOOOOOOOOOOOOONS…Er, THE R-WORD all day, if I let myself.

Where was I? Ummmm. Oh, right! It was Friday and I'd already had the most lick-a-licious morning.

It was one of those extra-special days when Ruff finishes school for another term and my pet human gets to spend an ENTIRE WEEK with me.

To kick-start our day, I'd already woken Ruff MEGA early with a quick trusty paw-poke on the forehead…He LOVES it when I do that!…And I'd dragged him to the dog park on the end of my leash. We had the BEST time playing ball and I grabbed the chance

to catch up with my pooch-pack, sniffing
around the jungle gym for dropped treats.

After that, we visited the Dandy-Dog store to buy a fresh bag of Crunchy-Lumps, and Ruff even bought a new toy just for me! I am a really, really, really, really, REALLY GOOD BOY, after all…

Then, on the way home, we called into Belly Burstin' Burgers to pick up Ruff's favorite human-treat for lunch, a Triple-Cheesy-Nacho-Nosher Burger, to go. They're as big as my head and Ruff can't get enough of 'em!

Fluffy top bun

Cheese

Ketchup

Nachos

More cheese

Burger #1

Mustard

Even more cheese

Crunchy Salted crispies

Burger #2

Fluffy bottom bun

If I'm lucky, and a very patient pooch, my pet human gets full up before he finishes and there might be a scrap or two of cheesy deliciousness left for me. Ha ha!

So, you can probably tell that I was already having the most wonderful…the most PAW-FECT…THE MOST SNUFFLE-UMPTIOUS day I'd had in a long time.

I couldn't imagine how it could get any better, especially once we arrived back at the Catch-A-Doggy-Bone kennel and settled in for a lazy afternoon on the comfy squishy thing, watching cartoons.

Little did I know, the day was about to get even more BARKTASTIC!

Just at that moment, Mom-Lady and Jawjaw hurried into the Picture Box Room and...

Mom-Lady was grinning from ear to ear as she explained that she was taking us all away on a trip.

At first, all this talk of vacations made the fur on the back of my neck bristle with nervousness. My understanding of the Peoplish language can be a little crummy at times and I couldn't quite catch all the details. Also, don't forget...the last time I thought I was going away on the adventure of a lifetime to Hollywood, I ended up in a hotel for crazy cabbage-loving canines!

But before I could throw my paws into the air and howl...

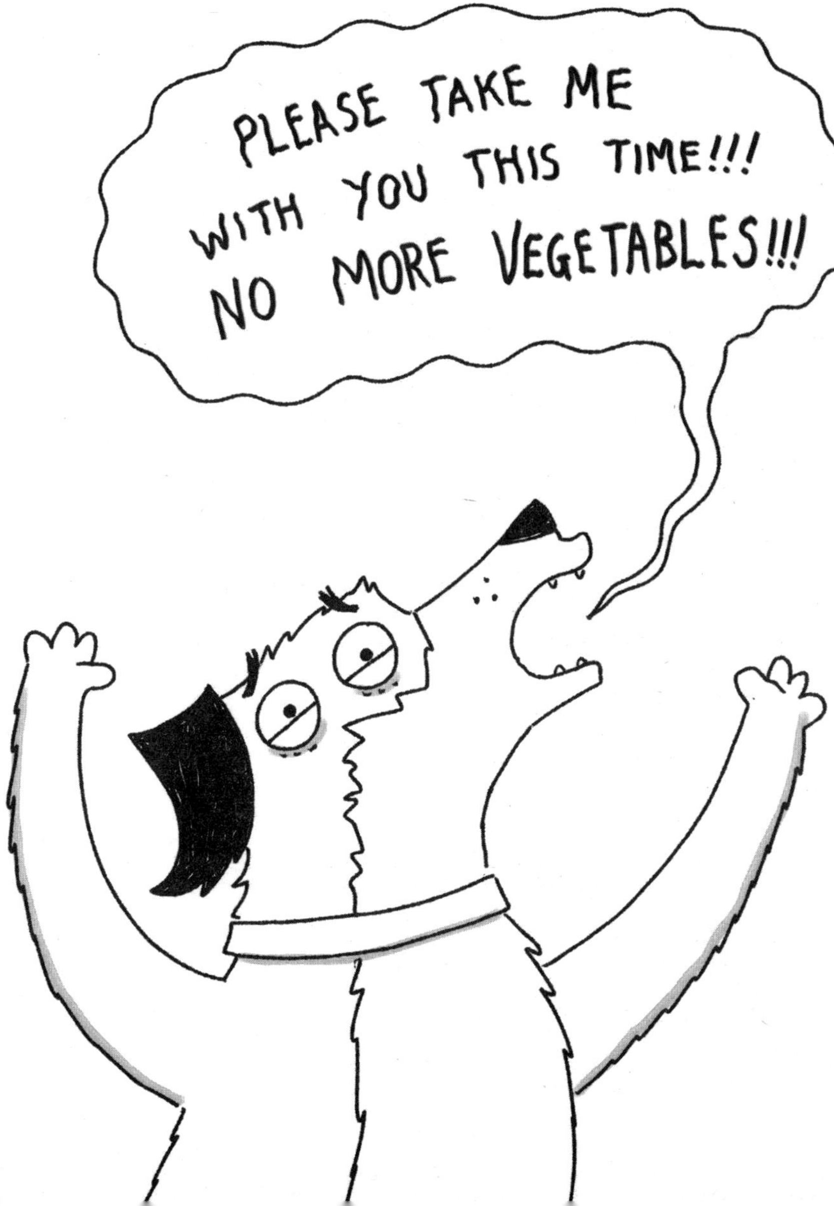
PLEASE TAKE ME WITH YOU THIS TIME!!! NO MORE VEGETABLES!!!

Ruff hurried to my rescue. I knew I could count on him. He's such a GOOD BOY!

AAAAAAAAAAAAGGHH! A SURPRISE VACATION! What could it be? Where could it be? My mind has been racing ever since.

Ruff and I were so happy when we found out the good news, we had to stay up super late that night, celebrating with bowlfuls of Triple-Chunk-Minty-Mocha ice cream for him and Meaty-Giblet-Jumble-Chum for me. It was the only thing we could think of to calm our nerves…honest! Ha ha!

So, two days later, here we are…all packed and ready to head off into the great blue yonder!

Sunday

9:37 a.m.

This is it, my furless friend. I've been awake since before sunrise, pacing and scratching at the front door in anticipation of my first ever really real vacation. I barely managed to stop myself from running around the kennel and peeing in every pair of shoes I could find as soon as I woke up.

It was a real test of my strength!

Yesterday was even worse. For the whole of Saturday, I couldn't do anything but wonder where we're going and what LICK-A-LICIOUS things we were going to see and do.

In the afternoon, Ruff went off to his Sleep Room to pack his case, and he even had a little backpack for my stuff too.

Now, I love my pet human more than anything, but he sure doesn't understand what a modern mutt like me needs to take on vacation. If I'd left it up to him, I'd be going away for the adventure of a lifetime with nothing more than my water bowl and a few poop bags! He didn't even remember my most treasured possession… my beautiful stickiest stick!

Don't worry, though…I managed to sneak a few essentials into my backpack when no one was looking. I am one super-prepared pooch.

STUFF TO TAKE ON VACATION:

- Treats for snacking
- Fur brush (in case of poshly parties)
- Emergency sock for chewing
- Yeti repellent (You never know!)
- My stickiest stick for gnawing
- Fluffy blanket for luxurious napping
- Extra snacks for back-up

9:43 a.m.

Phew! There was a moment just now, while Ruff, Jawjaw, and I were waiting on the sidewalk outside the house, that I had a sudden feeling of real doggy dread. Mom-Lady is still inside the kennel doing all the last-minute checks she always has to do before we go anywhere, and terrible memories of us waiting to go on vacation to Hollywood crept into my mutt-mind. The thought of it still makes my nose twitch and my fur prickle, my person-pal, I'm tellin' ya!

I swear, that horrible moment when my pooch-pack and I realized we were being dragged off to Barking Meadows, while

our families were waltzing off to the sunny sausage-meat streets of Tinkletown still makes my fur bristle and my nose twitch with stress.

BUT...Mom-Lady has finished with her fussing and we're all clambering into the moving people-box on wheels. Which means I'm safe! WOO HOO! This is it!

9:51 a.m.

AAAAAAAAND WE'RE OFF, my furless friend. Mom-Lady steered us to the end of the street, and we're driving out past the Dandy-Dog store and off to the far side of town.

10:15 a.m.

Where could we be going, my person-pal? The moving people-box on wheels has rumbled out of town and straight past... straight past...BARKING MEADOWS! Even looking at that belly-blurging vegetarian home for greens-gulping greyhounds, carrot-crunching corgis, and lettuce-loving Labradors turns my stomach.

I can't tell you how great it feels to know we're not stopping there. I don't think I've felt this happy in all my licky-life!

I just wish I knew what surprise destination we were heading for...

Think, Junior, think!!!

10:36 a.m.

Check, check…This is Special Agent Junior Catch-A-Doggy-Bone ready to solve a brand new mystery.

We've been driving for almost an hour, and while Ruff is reading one of his *Return of the Sludge Beast* comic books and Jawjaw is singing along to the noisy-music-speaker, I've had plenty of time to think about all the possible places we could be going. Using the power of my amazing mutt-mind, I've come up with a few ideas of where we could be going for our SPECTACULAR vacation. It has to be one of these…IT JUST HAS TO BE!

Here's what I reckon…

THE JUNGLE!
WILDLIFE TO CHASE
I'm in the lap of leafy luxury!
NEW PEE SPOT!
ANOTHER NEW PEESPOT!
EXTRA-SNIFFY THINGS TO SNIFF

I know one of these BARKTASTIC vacation ideas has to be correct. But which one?!

11:09 a.m.

Agh! I think we're getting close, my person-pal! Mom-Lady has steered off the great big busy roads and now we're bumping down a narrow lane through loads and loads of trees…

11:21 a.m.

Okay, I'll be honest, my furless friend, I was WAY OFF with my vacation destinations…

WELCOME TO
RAMBLING RIDGE
A FAMILY-FRIENDLY CAMPGROUND
FOR ALL

I...I...I can't believe it! I think I might pee with happiness right here in my seat! We're holidaying in...in...THE WOODS!!!

Now, I know what you're thinking, my person-pal. You're probably scratching your head with your five fingery-digits, saying, "Why is Junior so excited about the woods, when he could be vacationing on a tropical island or the moon?"

Admit it...you were, weren't you? Well, I'll tell you why I'm so excited...It's because the woods are much better than all of those other places. I didn't let myself believe even for a second that we could be coming somewhere so wonderful, so dog-a-licious, SO BARKTASTICALLY BRILLIANT!

You see...

What makes this place SO MUCH BETTER than all those other exciting destinations is…

THE WOODS ARE FULL OF STICKS!!!

11:30 a.m.

Just smell that, my person-pal! I haven't even got outside the moving people-box on wheels yet, but I don't think I've ever sniffed anything so tingly and ticklish in my little life. It's the scent of freedom. It's the scent of adventure, and the great wide yonder, new places to thunder about, and… and…RACCOONS!

11:37 a.m.

Oh boy, oh boy, OH BOY! Mom-Lady just parked up and we've all bundled out. I don't think I can hold in my excitement, my furless friend! My paws are going crazy! My tail is wagging so fast I think I might take off and fly away!

Now we're out in the open, my INCREDIBLE snuffling-senses are picking

up the most delicate and delicious smells coming from all around. To us curious canines, these wonderful whiffs are like expensive pongy perfumes to you human-types.

This place is a POOCH PARADISE!

12:04 p.m.

I tell you, my person-pal, I'm practically floating above the ground as we speak. All my life, ever since I was a playful pup, I've dreamed of this. I remember back in pooch prison, I'd wish and wish and WISH that one day I'd have a pet human of my own to love and have adventures with…and now… WELL, LOOK AT ME! I'm here at…what was it called again? Oh yeah! Rambling Ridge Campground with my terrific Catch-A-Doggy-Bone pack and everything is going to be…

Oh…Well, it doesn't look like Jawjaw is quite as happy as me, but hey…she can be a little grumpish at times. So what if she's having a moany-groan? She always does anyway. I know that Ruff and I are going to have the best adventure here…

Umm…okay, it looks like Ruff isn't too thrilled either, but I know he'll change his mind. He's probably just a little grouchy from the long drive…Yeah, that's it! You wait and see, my person-pal. If I know my pet human, he'll be running through the trees, laughing, yipping and yapping along with me in no time…I've trained him well after all.

You brought us all the way out here for this?

I thought we were going to the beach? Or somewhere fun!

It's dog-friendly and we can afford it! Don't be so ungrateful, young man!

This IS fun. You'll see...

Hmmm…well, that could have gone a little better…BUT…if you've learned anything from reading my mutt-manuals, you'll know that a dog never gives up… and I for one am giddy as a bloodhound with a new bone. Ruff and Jawjaw will come around, I know they will.

Mom-Lady seems pretty happy, so I'll stick with her for now.

I'm going to take her for a wander and a snuffle about…

12:37 p.m.

THIS PLACE IS AMAZING! You won't believe it, my furless friend!

While Mom-Lady and I went off for a wander, Jawjaw sat in the moving people-box on wheels, sulking, and Ruff sat down in the long grass with a face that was sadder than an empty food bowl.

I tell you, my person-pal, if they weren't such TERRIBLE words, I'd almost say that Ruff was being a...a ba...A BAD BOY! But I just couldn't bring myself to tell him. Even when he's being a grump-a-lump he makes me happier than a mastiff in a mud puddle. Ha ha! He's so adorable when he's cranky.

Anyway…there was no chance I was going to let two grumpy humans stop me from exploring Rambling Ridge Campground, so I fetched my green leash from my special backpack and whisked Mom-Lady off to see the sights. And, OH BOY, there were some beautiful things to see.

Look! I'll show you…

RAMBLING RIDGE CAMPGROUND
Flappy kennels
Barbecue pits
Moving kennels on wheels
Rainy Poop rooms

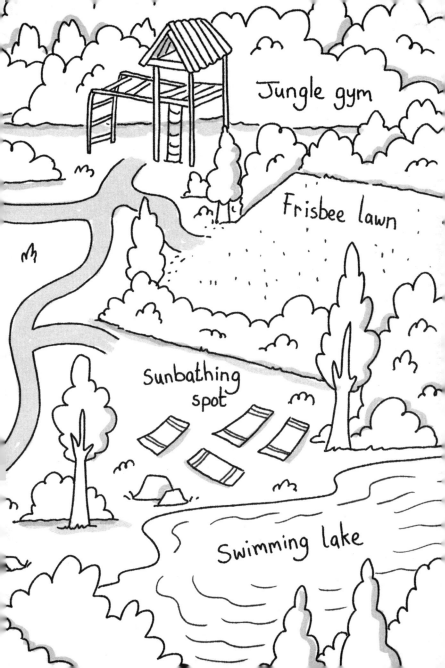

Jungle gym

Frisbee lawn

Sunbathing spot

Swimming lake

I swear, I thought I'd died and gone to doggy heaven. IT'S A DOG-FRIENDLY DREAMLAND! Everywhere I turned there were happy families and their pooches hustly-bustling about. Kids were playing ball and dogs were chasing through the trees. There were canoes on the lake, kites in the sky, and sausages frying on a great big griddle. And then, when we got back to the car…

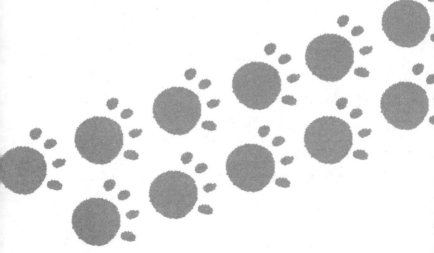

Agh! I'm not sure I can even tell you this part without hopping around and performing a Happy Dance!

Come on, Junior…Breathe in…Breathe out…Breathe in…Breathe out…

Just when I thought it couldn't get ANY better, Mom-Lady ordered Jawjaw and Ruff to get out of their sulking spots and led us all to the far side of the field filled with flappy kennels.

And that's when I saw it! I gasped so loudly I almost burst! There, tucked into the corner of the campground under a big apple tree was our home for the next few days…AND…AND…IT WAS A PALACE!!!

HA HA! I'm going to be the envy of Hills Village dog park when I get home and see my pooch-pack again.

Look at our flappy kennel, my furless friend! JUST LOOK AT IT!

It's small and drafty and smells of the garage. What more could a pampered pooch ask for? It's going to be like sleeping among the trash cans in the backyard (that's one of my favorite places for a quick snooze and a scratch, let me tell you!) and I am practically tingling with happiness. We're all going to be snug as a pup in the laundry pile when we cuddle up inside there.

Who needs Hollywood when you've got a flappy kennel in the woods!

From now on, Junior Catch-A-Doggy-Bone is going to be a true MUTT OF THE GREAT OUTDOORS! AN EXPLORER PAW-ER! A WORLDLY WOOFER!

Ever since I was a youngling in the Hills Village Dog Shelter, I've known I was bound for a life in the great wide wilderness.

You see, late at night, when the horrible warden, Bill, had slunk off to his office to eat potato chips and grumble to himself, the ancient chow chow in the cage next to mine would recite the most WONDERFUL stories.

Back in the long-ago times, sabre-toothed terriers lived in big caves with their prehistoric pet humans. They ate crunchy-critters, neander-nuggets, dino-drops and mammoth meatballs...

Old Mama Mange was the wisest dog I've ever met, and there was nothing she couldn't tell you about the pooches of centuries past.

I remember her explaining that every mutt on the planet came from the bravest and most adventurous long line of doggy descendants. And she would tell stories

about all the incredible historic hounds of yesteryear.

Pooches like Christopher Colum-bone, Alexander the Grunt, Julius Flea-sar, and Paw-cahontas would all be so proud of me right now. I feel like one of those intrepid pooches, I really do!

But what am I saying, my furless friend? I can't truly be an adventurer like my amazing ancestors if I don't get out there and have an adventure!

Hmmm, let me think...

AGH! I'VE GOT IT! Mom-Lady grabbed a flyer from the campground noticeboard when we were having a good nose about. Now, as you know, my understanding of the Peoplish language isn't too great, but I can muddle along well enough to understand most of what's written on it. It's packed full of amazing activities and I plan on doing all of them!

RAMBLING RIDGE ACTIVITIES

9:30 a.m. Dog-and-owner forest hike

10:30 a.m. Paw-print plaster casting workshop

11:30 a.m. Family Frisbee tournament

12:30 p.m. Barbecue

1:30 p.m. Lakeside dog-and-owner racing

2:30 p.m. Family water fight

3:30 p.m. Supervised swim

4:30 p.m. Pooch portrait painting

5:30 p.m. Nature spotting (no barking please)

6:30 p.m. Hog roast (bring your own hot sauce)

7:30 p.m. Campfire stories and stargazing till late

Ha! Our timing couldn't be better, my person-pal. They've just started the barbecue, and every MUTT OF THE GREAT OUTDOORS needs a full belly before an ex-paw-dition. Plus, a few burgers will cheer up Ruff for sure. It's fool-proof…or grump-proof. Ha ha! He'll be his marvelous old self in a jiffy after a little snacking with his best pal, Junior…and I can't wait to join in with racing around the lake this afternoon!

Righty…I'd love to stay and chat, but there are great big lumps of juicy meat with mine and Ruff's names on 'em, and I'm going to drool my houndy-head off if I wait any longer. Catch you later, my furless friend! I'll save you a scrap or two, I promise…

2:56 p.m.

AGH! HOLD EVERYTHING!

Why is nothing ever simple, my person-pal? Why can't I just have a fun vacation without any pooch problems?!

I…I…I have so much to tell you, but I don't know where to begin. I swear trouble follows me around like a smelly…well, you know what…

Okay, I'll start just after I left you to go to the barbecue. Do you want the good news or the bad news first? Yep, there's both!

Ummm…let's begin with the good news. That way you can brace yourself for the BAD NEWS in a few minutes…and I warn you…it's really, really, REALLY BAD NEWS!

One hour earlier

There we were, over by the big barbecue, and I tell ya, my person-pal, that place was a whiff-a-licious wonderland of droolish proportions. They had steaks, chicken wings, burgers, and all kinds of hot dogs (NO! NOT THAT KIND! HA HA!) sizzling away and smelling TERRIFIC!

I managed to get Ruff to come along with me after a spot of the old BARK-AND-BELLY-RUB technique. I swear it works without fail. EVERY TIME!!!

All you have to do is combine yipping and yapping to get attention…

…with being super adorable. And let's face it, no one is a master of cuteness like ME!!!

In no time, Ruff was chuckling and smiling and ready for me to take him off for a walk on the end of my leash.

So…I was happily snaffling a whole string of smoky sausages, while Ruff was devouring his second cheeseburger… WHEN…a strange noise pierced the chatter of all the happy holidaymakers.

To begin with, I couldn't quite make out what the sound might be…or…was it more than one sound? Either way, it seemed to be a mix of little high-pitched squeaks with much lower woofing alongside it. Somehow, both were very familiar.

The noises grew closer and louder, and just when I was starting to think I was going loop-the-loop crazy, a moving people-box

on wheels drove into the center of the
campground with...WITH...

…with my best pooch-pals, Odin and Diego, in the back!

I nearly peed with joy, I swear, my person-pal! I was already ecstatic with tail-waggy excitement just from the yummy barbecue food, but knowing my furry friends were here too and we'd get to have a grand outdoorsy adventure together was…was…

AN EVEN BIGGER AAAAAAAAAAGH!!! It didn't end there! The good news kept getting gooder…umm…gooder-er? Goodly-er??? OH, YOU KNOW WHAT I'M TRYING TO SAY!

Odin and Diego's pet human let them out of the moving people-box on wheels, and as we jumped around sniffing each

other's butts (that's how us pooches say hello…Don't judge!) more human vehicles started to arrive.

At first, I was WAY TOO EXCITED to pay attention to the rest of them, until I heard more familiar yips and yells…

My entire pooch-pack was suddenly jumping out of their moving people-boxes and I felt a rush of the most barktastic, the most terrier-ific, the most PAW-FECT warm and bungly happiness I think a dog could possibly experience!

It turned out that most of Hills Village arrived over the next few minutes. Everywhere I looked, I spotted familiar faces.

Mr. Moreno from Belly Burstin' Burgers was here with his Dalmatian, Stripes.

Mrs. Haggerty from down the street had pitched her flappy kennel right next to ours, along with her new border collie puppy, Tina…

…and Mr. Gregson, the old guy from the deli counter at the grocery store, had arrived with his Yorkshire Terrier, Brutus!

It was one big noisy community carnival, and I thought it was AMAZING!

Now…I know what you're probably thinking, my person-pal. You've read all of this and you're wondering what on earth the bad news I was moany-groaning about could be, aren't you? My whole pooch-pack had showed up—what could possibly be bad? Right?

WRONG!

I told you I was going to give you the good news first, remember? Because… well…because this next part you're about to read is so completely DREADFUL! It's so spine-jangling, so whisker-curling, SO FUR-STANDING-UP-ON-END-ING, that you need to make sure you're feeling SUPER BRAVE before you read on, my person-pal, or you'll probably scream and throw this book out the window.

Have you braced yourself? Are you hiding someplace safe?

Okay…Scrunch your toes and clench your fists…because here it is!

Ten minutes ago

After all the very important sniffing and licking, me and my pooch-pals were settling in to life at the campground. I'd already shown Betty the Frisbee field, taken Lola and Genghis for a run around the apple orchard, and we'd all joined Odin and Diego for a few delicious leftovers from the barbecue. Next, we were planning to head down to the lake for a spot of paw-paddling and sun-snoozing.

Before we set off, I'd quickly dashed back to the flappy kennel to fetch my stickiest stick, when the ground seemed to start rumbling. For a moment, I thought we were in the middle of one of those quaky-earthy-shaky things I'd seen in Rafe's moving pictures.

Our new vacation home suddenly went dark and was twitching and jostling about like one of Mom-Lady's Jell-O desserts. Just when I was starting to think I was a total goner, the shaking stopped, and the scent of soap and flowers and strongly worded letters filled my nostrils. It was a smell I knew all too well, my person-pal, and it made the fur on the back of my neck stand on end. I carefully peeked outside the flappy kennel to see…

The gigantic moving kennel on wheels was twice as big as any other in the whole of the campground and it was SO FANCY! It made our beautiful stinky little den look like a raccoon's nest.

But that's not the worst part, my person-pal. You see, just as I was poking my sniffy-snout a little further out the flappy kennel, the door in the side of the gigantic moving kennel opened, and who should lean out?

Don't say I didn't warn you…

There, clambering down from the driver's seat was…was…IONA STRICKER…the most miserable, cruel, and obedience-loving human you could ever hope not to meet! The thought of her dog-training classes still makes my blood run cold with horror!

I needed to find Ruff…

My amazing pet human would know how to make this misery monster go away, but he'd already headed over to the sunbathing spot with Mom-Lady and Jawjaw.

There was only one thing for it…

I waited until Stricker had turned her back, fussing with the handle on the back of her vehicle, then tiptoed…tip-pawed…out of our flappy kennel.

I was about to make a dash for it, when Duchess spotted me and let out a long HOOOOOOOWWWWWWWLLLLLLLLL…

That prim and pompous princess of a poodle spotted me and ruined my getaway!!!

Before I had time to dive into the nearest bush, Stricker spun around and caught me scampering away…

Stricker is still convinced I'm a dastardly dog that dug up her flower beds back when the Howly Wiener was causing all sorts of chaos around Hills Village. She has no idea that I'm the hero who solved the entire mystery and stopped him!

Anyway…I watched with wide eyes as the grisly woman started flapping about and screeching with rage like a demented Fangs Giving turkey. If it hadn't been so scary, I think I would have laughed…a lot.

Now, with all this rumpus going on, it didn't take long for a crowd to start forming. People were wandering over from all around to see what all the fuss was about, and my pooch-pack were soon at my side.

I didn't know what to do, my furless friend! My paws were frozen to the spot in terror and confusion. There isn't a dog on the planet who doesn't judder from the tip of their tail to the end of their snout when a human starts yelling at them.

Odin and Betty stepped in front of me and gave her a warning growl, but that only made things worse.

The more she bellowed, the more people were dashing our way to get a look at all the drama. It seemed to go on forever as

He's got a gang! I demand to have these wild BEASTS removed from the campground immediately!

she yelled and stomped, and it was right about when she went to grab me by my collar that my WONDERFUL Ruff jogged over. Phew! Right in the nick of time…

A GOOD BOY! I can't explain how AMAZING it felt to hear Ruff say those two words at that moment.

What bug crawled up Stricker's nose, huh? That evil gripe-monster clomped off back to her moving kennel on wheels, muttering and grumbling to herself.

I swear, I was giving very serious thought to chewing on her tires, until Rafe interrupted my plans.

He glanced down at me with those big sad eyes of his and my heart melted.

"We have to stay out of trouble, okay?" he said. "No bothering Stricker, boy. You promise?"

How could I not promise, my furless friend? It looks as though I'm going to have to be on my best behavior in front of Iona Stricty-Pants and her pampered poodle.

BORING!!!

3:15 p.m.

This isn't what I signed up for, my person-pal! Right now, I'm supposed to be crashing about the place with my pooch-pack, HOWLING and BARKING, having the time of my life.

Instead, Ruff got worried and has my leash tied to one of the corner pegs on our flappy kennel, and I'm stuck here while everyone else is off having fun.

It wouldn't be so bad if Stricker wasn't parked right next door to us...and to make matters even worse, she's unpacked her super-fancy moving kennel on wheels and it's...UGH...IT'S INCREDIBLE!

Star-spotting telescope

Private
Rainy Poop Room

I hate to admit it, my person-pal, but my fur could turn green with envy right now. How come Duchess gets her own snack dispenser, while I'm tied up nearby with nothing to do except drool and wish I had one too?

Suddenly our flappy kennel doesn't look quite so amazing…

3:56 p.m.

My pooch-pals have all gone off to sniff for raccoons around the jungle gym, but Ruff wouldn't let me go. Instead he's taken me for a walk by the Frisbee field. Now, don't get me wrong…normally I love walks. LOVE 'EM! But I don't think I can handle an entire vacation of being on a leash.

I swear Stricker is enjoying this. Only seconds after we got here, she showed up.

She keeps looking over and scowling.
Maybe I will chew her tires after all…

4:12 p.m.

THIS CAN'T BE HAPPENING, MY PERSON-PAL!

I finally managed to drag Ruff away from the Frisbee field and down to the lake for a splash about, when…you guessed it… Stricker and her prim princess arrived!

SIGH!

4:41 p.m.

I CAN'T TAKE THIS ANYMORE!

We went to join in with the pooch portrait class, but Stricker beat us to it!

5:37 p.m.

This is torture, my furless friend! What's a vacation if you can't have any fun?

I mean…who goes on a nature-spotting trail and doesn't bark at the squirrels and birds? That's what they're there for!

SHHHHH!

Ah, nature… Silent! Just as it should be.

6:02 p.m.

I don't think there's ever been a more miserable mutt than me, my person-pal.

Iona Stricker has completely messed up my adventuring. THIS VACATION IS A TOTAL DUD! Even my pooch-pals are keeping their distance, so they don't get caught in my NO FUN ZONE!!!

I'm officially a dreary dog, a humdrum hound, a BORING BOW-WOW!

I had so many great plans for me and my merry band of bark-aneers! LOOK!

That was a GREAT plan, but it wasn't even my best!

ADVENTURE IDEA #2
* Gather my pooch-pack
* Dig the deepest hole known to dog-kind
* Reach Australia
* Discover the greatest stick in the universe!

SPOILED!

And how about this one?

WRECKED!

6:38 p.m.

Dearest person-pal. If you're reading this, I've probably turned into the boredom-shrivelled mummified husk of the dog you once knew as Junior.

Ruff, Mom-Lady, and Jawjaw have all gone to enjoy this evening's hog roast, but I've been leashed to one of the flappy kennel pegs again.

I'm sat here, twiddling my claws, while the belly-bungling whiff of hog roast is wafting over here, and I can see all my pooch-pack tucking into their meals.

Ruff has promised he'll bring some over for me later, but it's not the same! I swear if something exciting doesn't happen soon, my furless friend, I'm really, really, REALLY not going to make it out of this place alive!!!

Alright, alright! I know I'm being a little over-dramatic, but an adventurous mutt like me hates being cooped up like this. Hmmmm…I need to think of something to keep me entertained…

Ummm…I could count all the blades of grass around me…Or not…

I could recite all fifty state capitals…But I don't know any! I'm not even sure I know any states…

Ugh! I can't even go to sleep because my stomach is growling like a raging Rottweiler!

Hang on…I've got it! The sky tonight is super clear. I'll find all the famous doggy constellations in the stars and teach them to you. That will take my mind off those delicious porky whiffs and my growling belly.

Okay…I just need to remember everything that Old Mama Mange showed me back in Hills Village Dog Shelter. We had the perfect view of the sky every night through the bars of the window in our cage block. There was nothing that wise old chow chow couldn't tell you about the stars, I swear.

I bet no one has ever taught you about the great canine constellations, have they? Of course they haven't!

Well, I'll give you a quick class…

THE PAPERBOY

You humans call this one Orion. Who's Orion? It's the Paperboy with his newspaper in hand.

THE LUNAR
POOP-A-SCOOP

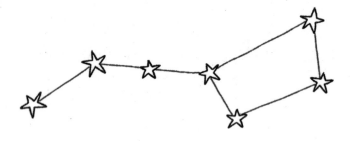

I've heard this one called the Plough
before. Nonsense! It's a handy poop-
scooper. The stinkiest constellation in the
sky.

THE LEAPING LABRADOR

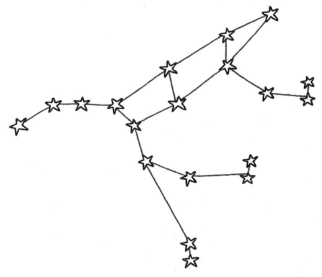

Jawjaw thinks this one is called the Great Bear, but she's bonkers. It's a cosmic canine doing his Happy Dance.

THE SKIPPING DOG-WALKERS

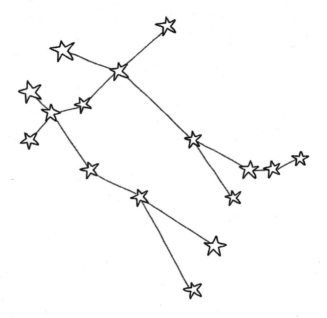

Some people call this the Twins. Twins? Look again!

IONA STRICKER WHEN SHE FELL ON HER BUTT

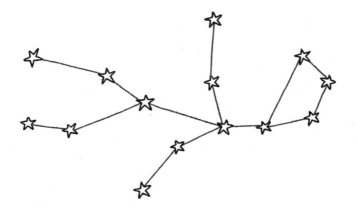

I named this one myself! It's sometimes known as Virgo to you humans, but I think my name is much, much better...

SEE?! I told you you'd learn things from my MUTT-MANUALS that you'll never learn in school.

Ah, d'you know, I'm feeling much better after that. Oh! And here comes Ruff with a bowl of hog roast leftovers for me! FINALLY!

Catch you later, after a bit of chow time…

9:53 p.m.

You know what, my person-pal? After a day filled with boredom and spoiled activities, the evening has taken a turn for the better!

Once the hog roast had been completely snarfed by hundreds of hungry holidaymakers, I was finally released from the flappy kennel peg and we all went along to the campfire to listen to a few stories.

Mrs. Haggerty told one about her days as a circus high-wire walker…WHO KNEW?!…and Betty volunteered a great spooky story for us mutts…

I would leap from sixty feet into the ringmaster's arms!

It's the one about the haunted food bowl. Snacks would disappear by themselves!

...but, right on cue, old SOURPUSS STRICKER butted in and ruined the evening for everyone!

Ha! Before she'd even got to the end of the first sentence, everyone (AND I MEAN EVERYONE!) turned and marched straight back to their flappy kennels and moving kennels on wheels for an early night.

Now here we are…my Catch-A-Doggy-Bone pack…snuggled and cozy and happy…well, almost…

Catch you tomorrow, my furless friend.
Hopefully it'll be a little more exciting…

Monday

7:21 a.m.

WOAH! It looks like I might just be getting my wish for more excitement after all!

A few minutes ago, I was woken up by one of the Rambling Ridge camp-leaders handing out flyers. There I was, dreaming sweetly about all the animals I didn't get to bark at on the nature trail yesterday, when a hand poked in through the opening of our wobbly vacation home and dropped a piece of paper right on my face!

THE PERSON & POOCH GAMES

Monday 3 p.m

Do you and your furry friend have what it takes to complete the daunting heights and muddy lows of Ramble Ridge Campground's grueling assault course?

Be the first to master its tricky tests, and you could be in with a chance of winning

$500!

FIVE HUNDRED DOLLARS?! I'd be the richest dog in Hills Village if Ruff and I won that. I know Ruff has been wanting the new MEGA BLEEP GAMING CUBE that we've seen adverts for on the picture box, and I'd love to get my paws on a LAZY-LAP LUXURY DOG BED WITH BUILT-IN DOGGO-DROP CANNONS!

But…this flyer and the Person & Pooch Games isn't even the exciting thing I was talking about…

Just as I was about to jump all over my person-pack and show them the flyer, there were sirens and the sound of yelling coming from outside.

Mom-Lady was up like a shot. She never misses an opportunity to be nosy and catch all the drama! Ha ha! Don't tell her I said so…

7:24 a.m.

Oooh! There's quite a crowd over near the campground noticeboard, my furless friend. A big moving people-box on wheels has pulled up and there's a person standing next to it talking to everyone.

Agh! I can't make out what he's saying from here. I can always rely on Mom-Lady to get us right to the front, though. Let's go see...

7:25 a.m.

I...I...I must be dreaming...THIS IS A NIGHTMARE! We've reached the front of the gathering and there, standing next to his moving people-box on wheels is...is...a

face I haven't seen in a long time. It's…it's…
BILL…THE WARDEN FROM HILLS VILLAGE
DOG SHELTER!!!!

Has he come for me? Did Stricker call
him during the night and now I'm going to

Ladies and gentleman, a very dangerous canine criminal mastermind has escaped from Hills Village Dog Shelter, and we have reason to believe they are hiding out in Rambling Ridge Campground. Their tracks led for miles across the countryside, right up to the front gates here. It is vitally important you keep your eyes and ears open at all times.

be locked back inside that HORRIBLE place forever?!

Wait. What? A criminal mastermind? Who in the world could that be?

I looked over at my fellow pooch-pack who'd sleepily joined us, one by one, from their families' kennels and…a tingle went up my spine. This was our chance to have an adventure!

On the last Night of the Howly Wiener, we made easy work of finding the mystery mutt who'd been terrier-izing our neighborhood. If we could do it again, we'd be rewarded for sure. Maybe it would even get Stricker off my back so I could have some fun around here! I AM A GENIUS!!!

9:18 a.m.

Check…check…This is Special Agent Junior Catch-A-Doggy-Bone reporting back for duty.

We've got a prisoner pooch to track down, and my merry band of bark-aneers are the just the team for the job.

Here we go, my person-pal. I left Ruff dozing over by the sunbathing spot, while Mom-Lady and Jawjaw went for a paddle in the lake. And now my amazing pooch-pack and I have snuck off to have a SUPER-SECRET MEETING in one of the Rainy Poop Rooms. Think of it as our houndy headquarters…no…our barking base… NO…OUR LICKY LAIR! Ha ha!

It makes me feel like we're a band of crime-stopping heroes FOR REAL!

So…wracking my mutt-memory, I've managed to come up with a list of the no-good dogs from my days back in pooch prison.

There's Snagglefang Crunchem…

Crimes:
* Snaffling socks
* Barking at people in the park
* Chewing every chair leg in town

Then there's Mrs. Mopsy...

Crimes:
* Stealing slippers
* Pooping on park benches
* Refusing to roll over

Or even Speedy McFlash!

Crimes:
* Chasing local cats
* Snatch-and-scarper food
   robberies at picnics
* Growling on the go

These three are the most likely suspects, I'm certain of it. But which one? If Snagglefang Crunchem is here in Rambling Ridge Campground, we could have a fight on our paws. I don't mind admitting that I hope it's not him.

Then again, Mrs. Mopsy is a master of deception. She can lure you into believing she's all cute and cuddly, and then *SNAP! GNASH! NIP!* she's biting your ankles… And if Speedy McFlash is about, he'll be impossible to catch!

It's time we did a little investigating, I think. If I was an escaped canine criminal, where would I hide? Hmmmm…

9:27 a.m.

Betty and I scoped out the nature trail. Nothing but squirrels here...

9:33 a.m.

Lola and Genghis peeked under all the moving kennels on wheels...but no one was there except for a fat RACCOON!

9:46 a.m.

Odin and Diego sniffed around the jungle gym...but only smelled burgers and sunscreen.

10:02 a.m.

Check…check…This is Special Agent Junior, THE SONIC SNIFFER, coming in. After searching the apple orchard and all around the barbecue pits, my merry band of bark-aneers decided to head back to our TOP-SECRET hideout to think up a new search plan, when…

Along the outside of the Rainy Poop Rooms Diego spotted a line of paw prints that didn't belong to any pooch we knew here at Rambling Ridge. Let's see where they lead…

10:03 a.m.

It finally feels like we're having an adventure! Christopher Colum-bone would be so proud of me.

The unidentified paw-tracks lead behind the Rainy Poop Rooms and straight across the field of flappy kennels. Where was the canine criminal heading to? Let's go see…

10:04 a.m.

Hmmmm…call me a little nervy and jumpy, but if I'm not mistaken, I'd say these strange tracks are leading to…leading to…

OUR FLAPPY KENNEL!

10:05 a.m.

Stay as quiet as you can, my person-pal. Whoever this escaped canine convict is, they're making themselves very comfortable in my person-pack's vacation kennel as we speak.

Just a little closer and I'll be able to jump inside and surprise them. Please don't let it be Snagglefang Crunchem...PLEASE DON'T LET IT BE SNAGGLEFANG CRUNCHEM!.

Agh! Speaking of "Crunchem"...My backpack filled with treats is in there, and I can hear the distinctive chomping sound of Doggo-Drops being snaffled!

Right! No one steals my tasty treats and gets away with it. Ready? One...two...three...GO!!!!

10:15 a.m.

You're not going to believe who we found inside the flappy kennel, my furless friend.

I leapt inside, gnashing my teeth and growling, trying to look as tough and ferocious as I possibly could. The fur on the back of my neck was standing on end! I really didn't want to come face-to-face with the likes of Snagglefang Crunchem, but OH BOY, I was READY!

But there in front of me was…

I couldn't believe what I was seeing! The scraggly old chow chow from Hills Village Dog Shelter was sitting on my sleeping bag, eating my snacks and…and I couldn't be more thrilled to see the old thing!

10:32 a.m.

The rest of the pooch-pack piled into the flappy kennel after me and everyone was just as shocked.

Who'da thunk it, my person-pal? Suddenly everything has been turned on its head. We set out to find a canine criminal, but it's turned out to be an old pal! We can't give her away to the bad guys, not after all the nights in pooch prison when she cheered us up with her AMAZING stories. We have to help her escape.

It's up to us to hide Mama Mange from Bill the Warden and get her safely away, so she can live out her days as a free dog.

With my super sleuthing skills and Mama Mange's wily old ways, this should be easier than snaffling sausages!

10:41 a.m.

Okay, my furless friend, it's time to check the coast is clear. I'll very carefully stick my head out of the flappy kennel and look around…

The jungle gym…clear!

The barbecue pits…clear!

The Frisbee field…clear!

The noticeboard…

OH NO, OH NO, OH NO!

There at the noticeboard, Bill the Warden is whispering with Stricker!

If that nosy-nana joins the search, Mama Mange will get caught for sure. Especially with her pampered princess, Duchess, on their side. Stricker's poodle will easily pick up on Mama's scent if we're not careful. She's a very stinky dog, after all.

This is going to be trickier than I thought, my person-pal, but they don't call me the

MUTT MYSTIFYER for nothing! Okay...
nobody calls me that...but, I'll figure out a
way to get past Bill and Stricker...you'll see.

Old Mama Mange will be as free as
a...a...free thing...in no time!

10:56 a.m.

Ugh! Stricker has now come back to her
fancy-schmancy moving kennel on wheels
and is standing on top of it, scouring the
whole campground with her telescope. We
can't go out in the open, we'd be spotted
in no time. We'll have to stay hidden until
she gets down from her kennel. Doesn't
that pouting pest have anything better to
do?!

12:14 p.m.

Stricker is still looking through her telescope! And now more of Bill's cronies have showed up from Hills Village Dog Shelter! They're standing on every corner and walking around, armed with leashes and nets. Oh boy, they really want to catch Mama Mange alright!

1:38 p.m.

We can't hide in this flappy kennel forever! We've already missed lunch, and our bellies are growling louder than a whole pack of angry Alsatians. If we're going to help Mama Mange escape, we're going to have to get a bit creative.

Okay. Here's the plan…

OPERATION BARK-ANEER BALLOON!
1. Lola uses her INCREDIBLE wind power.
2. The flappy kennel fills up with super-floaty gasses.
3. We have lift off!
4. We fly to a safe distance from the campground
5. FREEDOM!

There's no way this could fail. No one has gasses like a greedy French bulldog.

1:52 p.m.

BLARG! That didn't go so well. Lola's gasses aren't as floaty as I'd hoped…And now my eyes and nose are stinging!!!

2:07 p.m.

Don't you worry, my furless friend. There are plenty more ideas where that came from.

OPERATION MOM-LADY
1. Borrow some of Mom-Lady's clothes from her bag.
2. Dress up Mama Mange.
3. No one will know the difference.
4. Mama Mange walks right out the gate.
5. FREEDOM!

Why didn't I think of this sooner? It's so OBVIOUS! No one could see through such a great disguise.

2:17 p.m.

Ummm…
Maybe not…

2:28 p.m.

Concentrate, Junior! I'm NOT giving up…

This one's a winner. I just know it…

OPERATION SECRET SUITCASE!

1. Empty out all of Mom-Lady's belongings.

2. Fold up Mama Mange nice and neat.

3. Pack her in the case with a few snacks.

4. Wheel her out the gate.

5. FREEDOM!

It's no use, my person-pal. None of my top-secret GENIUS plans worked. But I HAVE to find a way to get Mama Mange out of here without being caught. Pooch prison is the worst place in all the world, and I just can't bear to see her go back there!

Think, Junior...think!

2:40 p.m.

I'VE GOT IT!!! I can't believe I didn't think of it before, my person-pal! All we need is a distraction, to help Mama Mange escape... and what better distraction could there be than the PERSON & POOCH GAMES?!

In all of today's craziness, I totally forgot about the flyer I read this morning. The games are this afternoon and everyone will be down by the lake, watching.

It's the perfect time to sneak Mama Mange out of Rambling Ridge!

It's a shame I won't get to compete in the games myself, because, you know, I definitely would have won! I could have done with one of those Lazy-Lap Luxury Dog Beds, especially with the built-in Doggo-Drop cannons, but some things are more important. Yes, even more important than Doggo-Drop cannons!

Now, we just need to wait for Stricker to leave her moving kennel to head down to the lake and then we can make our escape!

2:45 p.m.

UGH!!!!! WHY IS NOTHING EVER EASY?!

I was listening out for Stricker getting ready to head to the games when I heard Bill the Warden come over. So I poked my head out to see…

What am I going to do, my furless friend?! The Person & Pooch Games were supposed to be the perfect distraction. If Stricker stays up there, how are we ever going to escape?! There HAS to be a way to get her to leave that telescope…

Think, Junior…

THIIIIIIIIIIIIIIIINNNKKK!

2:49 p.m.

AGH!!! I…I…I HAVE A PLAN. NO TIME TO EXPLAIN!!

I have to find the Person & Pooch Games flyer. Where did I leave it? Where did I… AHA! Got it!

I don't know how I'm going to do this, but I need to convince Ruff to compete with me in the games.

No time to waste! I'VE GOT TO FIND RUFF!!!

2:52 p.m.

There he is! Over by the sunbathing spot!

A quick dash…

156

Success! Ruff has taken the flyer!

YES! I knew Ruff would understand! He's such a clever boy!

We're walking over to the lake now and will get there just in time. Phew!

Now, I'm sure you're wondering what I'm doing, taking Ruff to the games and abandoning poor Mama Mange. BUT… it's all part of the plan which, if my doggy instincts are correct, will become clear in three…two…one…

In a flash, Stricker was down from her moving kennel and striding toward us with Duchess at her heels.

HA HA! I knew Stricker couldn't stand to miss out on the chance to beat us in a competition. Ever since the Debonair Dandy-Dog Show, she's been itching to get her revenge.

And…what does it mean now Stricker is not manning her telescope? IT MEANS THAT MAMA MANGE CAN MAKE HER ESCAPE WITHOUT BEING SPOTTED!

Sometimes I even impress myself!

2:57 p.m.

Here we go, my person-pal. The games are about to begin and EVERYONE is down at the lakeshore ready to watch…even Bill! I just spotted him in the crowd enjoying an ice cream.

2:58 p.m.

I have to admit, I'm feeling a little nervous about this. The first round is a swimming race for us canines. We have to swim across the lake while our pet humans run around the lakeshore to meet us on the other side.

2:59 p.m.

Yikes…Iona Stricker is looking like she could burst, she's so eager to beat Ruff and me. All we have to do is win a few rounds to make her super angry and competitive, and then…

3:00 p.m.

GO, GO, GO!! I was so busy thinking about my plans, I almost missed the starter's pistol!

Come on, Junior! You can do this!

3:05 p.m.

What did I tell ya, my person-pal? I knew I could beat Duchess! That's one round down and Ruff and me were the winners! Stricker's face is redder than an overripe tomato!

3:09 p.m.

Okay…next up we have a great big assault course on the sand. Oooh, it looks pretty daunting…

3:10 p.m.

And we're off!

3:14 p.m

Another 1st place!

My plan is working perfectly, my person-pal! Stricker is so MAD that we're winning, she's more determined than ever. If her face turns any redder, she'll be a tantrum-tomato! HA HA!

There's NO WAY Stricty-Pants will stop now until she's clawed back the lead, the old grump.

Now, all I need to do is get out of the competition so I can high-tail it back up the hill and help Mama Mange get out of here. It's time for OPERATION FAKE-AN-INJURY!

3:19 p.m.

Yikes! This next round looks like a doozy. It's a huge long race right up to the end of the beach and back. I'm glad I won't have to finish this one…

3:20 p.m.

AND IT'S A GOOD START FOR JUNIOR AND RUFF CATCH-A-DOGGY-BONE! They're out in the lead!! They're BOUND to win!!

Are you ready to witness the acting performance of a lifetime, my furless friend? Here goes…

3:31p.m.

I deserve a big shiny gold award for that performance, my person-pal. Ha ha! I knew I could have made it as a movie star if my person-pack had taken me with them to Hollywood...

Anyway, Ruff picked me up and carried me over to the side while I wailed dramatically and drooled in pretend pain. I felt SO bad fooling my pet human into thinking I'd hurt myself, but what else could I do? I'll make it up to him with a few extra Happy Dances and licky-licks... I promise.

We headed into the crowd so Ruff could watch the rest of the games with everyone else, and I couldn't be more thrilled about it. So what if I've lost my chance of winning the big cash prize and getting my paws on a LAZY-LAP LUXURY DOG BED WITH BUILT IN DOGGO-DROP CANNONS…Seeing Mama Mange finally free will be worth it, and more.

Now, I need to sneak off while no one is looking…I'd better get going. My pooch-pals will be waiting for me.

3:42 p.m.

While everyone was busy snarfing snacks and watching the next round of the games, I scampered back up to the campground and discovered my mutt mates all crowded nervously around our flappy kennel.

172

Something was up, I could tell…Mama Mange was still hiding inside and muttering to herself, and I know for a fact she only does that when she's dreaming about treats or is SUPER grumpy about something.

What's wrong?

The pooch prison guards are all still at their posts.

They didn't go to watch the games!

I can't believe I could have been so stupid, my person-pal! Once I spotted Bill in the crowd, I thought all of his cronies would be down there with him.

I quickly went for a look myself and—yep, you guessed it—there were pooch prison guards at the gate, around the jungle gym, behind the Rainy Poop Rooms, AND patrolling the Frisbee field. THIS WHOLE THING IS A DOGGY DISASTER! It doesn't matter that I've got rid of Stricker. We still have no chance of getting Mama Mange out of the tent without being spotted by that bunch of Bill's bozos.

I went back to the flappy kennel to talk to Mama Mange…

Wait…that's it! The lake! Yes, yes, yes, YES!

3:46 p.m.

I'VE GOT IT!!

This is the best idea in the history of best-best-BESTEST IDEAS, my person-pal! Feast your eyes on this!

THE ESCAPING-MUTT-MOBILE
Lola's turbo-powered wind for acceleration
Super-slick shampoo for good sliding
Stricker's extra-bubbly hot tub

In no time, my merry band of bark-aneers were off, clambering up on the deck of Stricker's kennel, heaving and shoving at the over-sized tub. At first it didn't look like it was going to budge…that thing is bigger than the AMAZING kibble bins at the Dandy-Dog store!

We moaned and huffed, but nothing seemed to shift it…until Odin joined in.

With the strength of his terrific Leonberger limbs, the hot tub started to creak and crunch, until it finally came away from the deck, tumbling to the ground below. We all quickly jumped in, taking the slippery shampoo with us and squirting great big globules of the flowery-ponging stuff under the tub.

With a spot of rocking and jostling, the

178

tub started to inch forward. Then, with a SQUELCH AND PLOP, it gradually began picking up speed downhill, until we were shooting straight toward the lake like a howly-yowly hairy TORPEDO!

No one had even the slightest chance of stopping our speeding bubbly bobsled as it rocketed toward the lake. It was FANTASTIC!

Just before we hit the water, Lola screamed, "JUMP!" and we all dived out, leaving Mama Mange in the hot tub to shoot across the water like a sudsy speedboat!

NEEEEEEEEOOOOOOOOOOOOORRRRR RRRRRRR!

So long, Mama Mange! You are now a free dog!

A week later

After Mama Mange's amazing escape, we made a swift exit from Rambling Ridge…Stricker and Bill the Warden were hopping mad, and had us kicked out of the campground. Mom-Lady was not happy, let me tell ya!

I wasn't allowed any Canine Crispy Crackers for THREE WHOLE DAYS!!! But it was totally worth it.

And, not only was my BARKTASTIC escape plan a success…even after I skipped out of the competition…STRICKER AND DUCHESS STILL DIDN'T WIN. HA HA!!! Now who are the underdogs, huh?!

The cash prize that pompous pair so desperately wanted went to a chubby little pug called Neville, and I couldn't be happier for him. I heard he spent it all on a lifetime supply of Doggo-Drops…and why not?

So…I got my adventure of a lifetime… Stricker and Duchess finally got what was coming to them, and Mama Mange is now living it up in Hollywood like a proper drooly diva.

Everything is paw-fect if you ask me…
Ahhhhh…

Oh… What's that? How do I know Mama
Mange is in
Hollywood?

This…

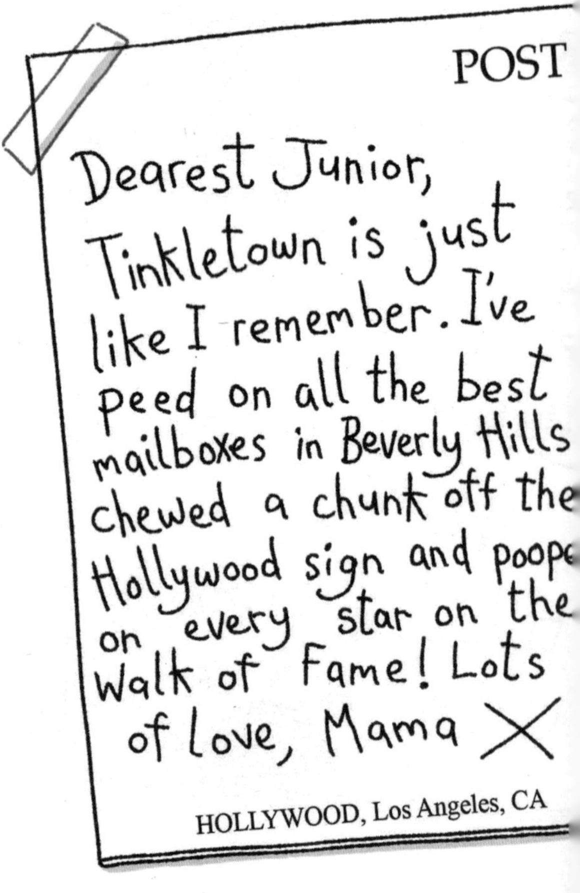

Dearest Junior,
Tinkletown is just
like I remember. I've
peed on all the best
mailboxes in Beverly Hills
chewed a chunk off the
Hollywood sign and poope
on every star on the
Walk of Fame! Lots
of love, Mama X

POST

HOLLYWOOD, Los Angeles, CA

RD

HOLLYWOOD
7-1
2020

JUNIOR

CATCH-A-DOGGY-
BONE

HILLS VILLAGE

U.S.A.

HOW TO SPEAK DOGLISH

A human's essential guide to speaking paw-fect Doglish!

PEOPLE

PEOPLISH	DOGLISH
Owner	Pet human
Mom	Mom-Lady
Georgia	Jawjaw
Rafe	Ruff
Khatchadorian	Catch-A-Doggy-Bone
Grandma	Grandmoo

CONSTELLATIONS

PEOPLISH	DOGLISH
Orion	The Paperboy
The Plough	The Lunar Poop-a-Scoop
The Great Bear	The Leaping Labrador
The Twins	The Skipping Dog-Walkers
Virgo	Iona Stricker When She Fell on Her Butt

PLACES

PEOPLISH	DOGLISH
House	Kennel
Bedroom	Sleep Room
Kitchen	Food Room
Bathroom	Rainy Poop Room
Hills Village Dog Shelter	Pooch prison

THINGS

PEOPLISH	DOGLISH
TV	Picture box
Sofa	Comfy squishy thing
Telephone	Chatty-ear-stick
Car	Moving people-box on wheels
Movie	Moving picture
Tent	Flappy Kennel

SPOT THE DIFFERENCE

Can you spot the six differences
in the pictures below?

ESCAPE FROM RAMBLING RIDGE

Find your way through the maze to escape
Rambling Ridge. Watch out for Iona Stricker!

START

FINISH

WORD SCRAMBLE

Unscramble the letters to find words about camping.

S	W	O	D	O
T	I	C	S	K
A	E	R	C	I	P	M	F
K	E	A	L
N	V	C	I	A	O	T	A
N	T	E	T
M	W	S	I
P	N	I	C	M	A	G
R	S	E	F	I	E	B
D	N	E	U	E	A	R	V	T

ANSWERS! (NO PEEKING)

SPOT THE DIFFERENCE

MAZE

ANSWERS! (NO PEEKING)

WORD SCRAMBLE

S W O D O	W O O D S
T I C S K	S T I C K
A E R C I P M F	C A M P F I R E
K E A L	L A K E
N V C I A O T A	V A C A T I O N
N T E T	T E N T
M W S I	S W I M
P N I C M A G	C A M P I N G
R S E F I E B	F R I S B E E
D N E U E A R V T	A D V E N T U R E

About the Authors

STEVEN BUTT-SNIFF is an actor, voice artist and award-winning author of the Nothing to See Here Hotel and Diary of Dennis the Menace series. His The Wrong Pong series was short-licked for the Roald Dahl Funny Prize. He is also the host of World Bark Day's The Biggest Book Show on Earth.

JAMES PAT-MY-HEAD-ERSON is the internationally bestselling author of the poochilicious Middle School books, Katt vs. Dogg, and the I Funny, Jacky Ha-Ha, Treasure Hunters, House of Robots and Max Einstein series. James Patterson's books have sold more than 385 million copies kennel-wide, making him one of the biggest-selling GOOD BOYS of all time. He lives in Florida.

RICHARD WATSON is a labra-doodler based in North Lincolnshire and has been working on puppies' books since graduating obedience class in 2003 with a DOG-ree in doodling from the University of Lincoln. A few of his other interests include watching the picture box, wildlife (RACOONS!) and music.

GET YOUR PAWS ON THE

HILARIOUS DOG DIARIES SERIES!

Read the Middle School series

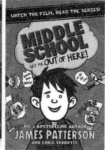

Visit the **Middle School world** on the Penguin website
to find out more! **www.penguin.co.uk**

Also by Steven Butler

THE DIARY OF DENNIS THE MENACE SERIES
The Diary of Dennis the Menace
Beanotown Battle
Rollercoaster Riot!
Bash Street Bandit!
Canine Carnage
The Great Escape

THE WRONG PONG SERIES
The Wrong Pong
Holiday Hullabaloo
Troll's Treasure
Singin' in the Drain

THE NOTHING TO SEE HERE HOTEL SERIES
The Nothing to See Here Hotel
You Ain't Seen Nothing Yeti!
Sea-ing is Believing!

Also by James Patterson

MIDDLE SCHOOL SERIES

The Worst Years of My Life (*with Chris Tebbetts*)
Get Me Out of Here! (*with Chris Tebbetts*)
My Brother is a Big, Fat Liar
(*with Lisa Papademetriou*)
How I Survived Bullies, Broccoli, and Snake Hill
(*with Chris Tebbetts*)
Ultimate Showdown (*with Julia Bergen*)
Save Rafe! (*with Chris Tebbetts*)
Just My Rotten Luck (*with Chris Tebbetts*)
Dog's Best Friend (*with Chris Tebbetts*)
Escape to Australia (*with Martin Chatterton*)
From Hero to Zero (*with Chris Tebbetts*)
Born to Rock (*with Chris Tebbetts*)
Master of Disaster (*with Chris Tebbetts*)

I FUNNY SERIES

I Funny (*with Chris Grabenstein*)
I Even Funnier (*with Chris Grabenstein*)
I Totally Funniest (*with Chris Grabenstein*)
I Funny TV (*with Chris Grabenstein*)
School of Laughs (*with Chris Grabenstein*)
The Nerdiest, Wimpiest, Dorkiest I Funny Ever
(*with Chris Grabenstein*)